BUS
STOP

For Maisie, with love
J.C.

First published in Great Britain in 2011 by Gullane Children's Books
185 Fleet Street, London, EC4A 2HS
Text and illustrations © Jane Cabrera 2011
First published in the United States by Holiday House in 2011
All Rights Reserved
HOLIDAY HOUSE is registered in the U.S. Patent and Trademark Office.
Printed and Bound in March 2011 at Shenzhen Fuweizhi Printing Ltd.,
Longhua Town, Baoan District, Shenzhen, China.
www.holidayhouse.com

First American Edition
1 3 5 7 9 10 8 6 4 2
Library of congress cataloging-in-Publication Data
Cabrera, Jane.
The wheels on the bus / Jane Cabrera. — 1st American ed.
p. cm.
Summary: In this version of the classic song, animal passengers roar,
flap, and chatter while riding a bus.
ISBN 978-0-8234-2350-7 (hardcover)
1. children's songs—Texts. [1. Buses—Songs and music. 2. Songs.] I. Title.
PZ8.3.cl22Wh 2011   782.42—dc22   [E]   2011000120

The Wheels on the Bus

Jane Cabrera

"All aboard, off and we go...."

Beep beep!

Holiday House / New York

The wheels on the bus go round and round,
Round and round, round and round.

The wheels on the bus go round and round,
All day long!

The Lion on the bus goes

Roar, roar, **roar,**
Roar, roar, **roar,**
Roar, roar, roar.

The Lion on the bus goes

Roar, roar, **roar,**

All day long!

The flamingos on the bus go
Flap, flap, flap,
Flap, flap, flap,
Flap, flap, flap.
The flamingos on the bus go
Flap, flap, flap,
All day long!

The Zebra on the bus goes
Chomp, chomp, chomp,
Chomp, chomp, chomp,
Chomp, chomp, chomp.

The Zebra on the bus goes
Chomp, chomp, chomp,
All day long!

The monkeys on the bus go
Chatter, chatter, chatter,
Chatter, chatter, chatter,
Chatter, chatter, chatter.

The monkeys on the bus go
Chatter, chatter, chatter,
All day long!

The hyena on the bus goes
Ha, ha, ha,
Ho, ho, ho,
Hee, hee, hee.

The hyena on the bus goes
Ha, ho, hee,
All day long!

The crocodile on the bus goes

Snap, snap, snap,

Snap, snap, snap,

Snap, snap, snap.

The crocodile on the bus goes
Snap, Snap, Snap,
All day long!

The chameleon on the bus plays
Hide-and-seek,
Hide-and-seek, hide-and-seek.

The chameleon on the bus plays
Hide-and-seek,
All day long!

Quietly now....

The bush babies on the bus go
Snore, Snore, Snore,
Snore, Snore, Snore,
Snore, Snore, Snore.

The bush babies on the bus go
Snore, Snore, Snore,
So shhh, shhh, shhh!

The animals on the bus say,
"Are we there yet?
Are we there yet? Are we there yet?"

The animals on the bus say,
"Are we there yet?"
All day long!

And the driver
on the bus says, . . .

"Yes!
Come on, everyone,
Let's get off the bus.

Now it's time to . . .

SPLASH! SPLOSH!
ALL day long!"

The Wheels on the Bus